What Will
Emily Do?

GILLIAN CROSS

What Will Emily Do?

Illustrated by Paul Howard

MAMMOTH

To Naomi

Extract from *Farmer Duck*
Text copyright © 1991 Martin Waddell
Illustrations copyright © 1991 Helen Oxenbury
Published by Walker Books Limited, London

First published in Great Britain 1994
by Methuen Children's Books Ltd
Published 1995 by Mammoth
an imprint of Reed International Books Ltd
Michelin House, 81 Fulham Road, London SW3 5RB
and Auckland, Melbourne, Singapore and Toronto

Reprinted 1995, 1996

Text copyright © 1994 Gillian Cross
Illustrations copyright © 1994 Paul Howard

The right of Gillian Cross to be identified as author of
this work has been asserted by her in accordance with
the Copyright, Designs and Patents Act 1988

ISBN 0 7497 2392 0

A CIP catalogue record for this title
is available from the British Library

Printed and bound in Great Britain
by Cox & Wyman Ltd, Reading, Berkshire

Contents

Chapter 1

Monday
Ducks

Matthew couldn't wait to start school. All through the summer holidays, he dreamed about writing and sums and learning to read. He thought about school all the time. But he never wondered what Emily would do while he wasn't there.

Not until the day he actually started.

That morning, she woke him up by bouncing on his chest, shrieking. 'School today! Can I play with your spaceship while you're not here?'

Matthew sat up and pushed her off. 'No, you can't.' The spaceship was made out of an enormous cardboard box, covered with kitchen foil, and it was his favourite thing.

'Play with your own toys.'

Emily looked cunning. 'If I do, will you read me a book when you come home from school?'

Matthew hesitated. He wasn't sure how much reading they'd learn on the first day. But he ought to learn enough to manage one of Emily's books. They were only short.

'*Please!*' said Emily.

'Well – all right.'

Emily beamed and bounced out of the room.

She was still bouncing when they walked to school, and every time she saw someone she knew, she shouted, 'Matthew's going to read me a book!'

Matthew walked more slowly, beside Mum. At the school gates, she gave his hand a squeeze. 'Look, there's Mrs Barton. Remember visiting her class last term? And there's Kirsty and Abigail. And Jason.'

'Jason's silly,' said Matthew.

He hung back, but Emily bounced straight up to Mrs Barton.

'Matthew's going to read me a book!'

Mrs Barton smiled. 'Hallo, Matthew. Would you like to go and find your peg? It's got a picture of a duck on it.'

'I'll find it!' Emily said. She bounced past Matthew, into the cloakroom. 'Here it is!'

The duck was white, with a yellow beak, and there was writing underneath it. *Matthew Gardner*. They were the only words Matthew could read properly. The next peg had a lion, and Jason was hanging his coat on it.

'Hello,' he said. 'Your lunch box goes up there.' He knew all about school, because his sister was seven. 'And you've got a drawer in the classroom with the same picture as your peg.'

'A duck!' screeched Emily.

She ran on, ahead of Matthew and Mum. By the time they caught her up she was yelling, 'Here it is!'

Matthew scowled and pushed her out of the way. 'It's *my* drawer. Don't poke your nose in.'

'I was only trying to help!' Emily said fiercely. She kicked his ankle.

Mum grabbed Emily's hand. 'Let's have a look round, shall we?'

But Emily didn't just look. She picked up the dolls in the Wendy House. She fiddled with the jigsaws and the Lego. And when they got to the book corner, she started taking books off the shelves.

'No!' said Mum.

She tried to pull her away, but Emily held on to the bookshelves and screamed.

'I want to read! Like Matthew! I want a book!'

'Be quiet!' hissed Matthew. 'Mrs Barton's coming!'

He thought she was coming to tell them off. But she wasn't. She smiled and crouched down beside Emily.

'Don't worry. You'll get a book. Matthew's going to choose one later on, to bring home.'

Emily stopped, in the middle of a scream. 'Really?'

'Really,' said Mrs Barton. 'All the children do it.'

Emily sniffed and gave her an enormous smile. Then she caught hold of Mum's hand. 'Let's go to playgroup now.'

Mum grinned with relief. 'Goodbye, Matthew.'

'I . . .' Suddenly Matthew felt very strange. 'Mum . . .'

'The other children are sitting on the carpet,' Mum said. 'Go on. You'll have a lovely day.'

'But . . .' Matthew looked at Emily's hand, holding on to Mum's. 'What will Emily do?'

'Emily?' said Mum. She blinked.

'Yes. After playgroup. What will she *do*?'

'She'll be all right.'

'But she might –' She might play with his spaceship. She might do *anything*. And he wouldn't know, because he'd be at school.

Mum looked across at the children sitting on the carpet. Then she looked back at Matthew. 'What do you *want* Emily to do?'

How could he think? Emily always did the same as he did. But she couldn't today, because . . .

Yes, she *could*!

'She can go to the library! I'm going to choose a book at school, so if she chooses one there – she'll be doing the same as me.'

'Yes!' said Emily. She jumped up and down and shouted. 'I'll choose a book! And you can read it to me, Matthew!'

She bounced off happily, holding Mum's hand, and Matthew went to sit on the carpet. He felt happy as well, until Jason leaned over and whispered, 'You can't read.'

'I'm going to learn,' Matthew said. 'That's what you do at school.'

'But it takes years and years!' Jason turned round and grinned at everyone else. 'Matthew thinks he can learn to read in *one day*!'

'I don't!' Matthew went pink. 'I never said –'

But it was too late. Everyone was laughing, and Jason was saying the same thing, over and over again.

'He thinks he can learn in one day! *One day*!'

Chapter 2

Monday

In One Day!

Jason kept the joke going all day. Mrs Barton made him be quiet in the classroom, but at playtime he dragged Matthew over to his big sister, Marie.

'Matthew thinks he's going to learn to read in one day! He said he'd read a book to Emily after school!'

Matthew went red. 'I didn't!'

But Marie was already giggling and whispering the story to her friends. 'He thinks he can learn to read in *one day*.'

By lunch time, every child in the school knew what Jason had said. People kept pointing at Matthew, or waving bits of writing at him.

'Read this! Go on!'

Matthew stared miserably at the words. He really *had* thought he was going to learn some reading today. But they hadn't done any yet. Only drawing and singing.

After lunch Mrs Barton said they could have 'Choosing Time', and Matthew went up and whispered in her ear.

'Can I learn to read? Just a few words?'

She just smiled. 'There's lots of time for that. Why not go and play Lego with David? He's only just moved here, and he doesn't know anyone.'

There isn't lots of time! Matthew wanted to

yell. *I've got to learn by home time*. But he didn't dare. So he went and sat beside David.

That wasn't too bad. David didn't talk much, but they built an enormous castle. And then Mrs Barton said, 'Now you can choose a book to take home.'

'To *read*,' whispered Jason, looking at Matthew.

Some people laughed, but David didn't. He pushed his chair back and nodded at Matthew.

'Come on. Let's get our books.'

The book Matthew really wanted had a white duck on the cover – just like the duck on his peg. But it had quite a lot of words, as well. So he left it on the shelf, and picked a dull-looking book about a little blue steam engine because it was short.

Maybe he could still learn enough words to read *that* to Emily.

But he hadn't realised how late it was. As soon as they'd finished choosing the books, Mrs Barton told them all to sit down on the carpet again. 'There's just time for a story before you go home.'

Matthew's mouth fell open. It was home time already – and he hadn't learnt to read a single word.

Mrs Barton smiled. 'Don't worry, Matthew. You'll be coming back again tomorrow. Now how about finding a nice story for us?' She waved her hand at the bookshelves.

Matthew gulped and pointed at the duck book.

'*Farmer Duck*?' Mrs Barton looked pleased. 'That's one of my favourites. Bring it over.'

Matthew gave her the book and sat down, close to her chair. Maybe, if he watched very carefully while she was reading he'd see how she did it. Then he could work out how to read the little blue engine book. He leaned sideways and peered at the black letters.

Mrs Barton looked at him. For a moment, he thought she was going to send him away, but she didn't. She turned back to the book and began to read.

'*There once was a duck who had the bad luck to live with a lazy old farmer . . .*'

She read the story twice, and Matthew stared at every word, watching how the story fitted the pictures, and where she turned the pages. After the second time, he could have recited it all over again, all by himself. For a few seconds, he actually thought he *might* have learnt to read.

Then he peeped into the little blue engine book. And he still couldn't understand any of *those* words.

He trailed out of school, hoping the other children had forgotten all about his reading. But they hadn't. The playground was full of children crowding round Mum and Emily.

'Come on, Matthew!' yelled Marie. 'Let's hear you read!'

'Yeah, come on!'

Mum looked at Matthew. 'I don't think –' she began.

But she didn't have a chance to finish. Emily bounced up to him, holding out her library book.

'I did the same as you!' she yelled. 'I chose a book! Read it to me!'

'I –' Matthew didn't know what to do. He couldn't read anything, but if he said so, everyone would laugh at him.

'Read it!' Emily said. She jabbed him in the stomach with the book.

Matthew took it out of her hands, to stop her jabbing, and swallowed hard. 'I can't –'

Then he looked down at what he was holding.

'I chose it on purpose,' Emily said proudly. 'Because of your peg and your drawer.'

Matthew smiled at the little white duck on the cover of the book. Then he opened it and began, in a very loud voice, '*There once was a duck who had the bad luck to live with a lazy old farmer . . .*'

He told the story all the way through, to the very end. And then he went home and flew to Mars in his spaceship.

Chapter 3

Tuesday

This is My Family!

Next morning, Matthew woke up and saw Emily standing beside the spaceship. She was peering through the porthole.

'No!' he said. 'Leave it alone!'

Emily stuck her tongue out. 'You won't be able to stop me when you're at school.' She grinned wickedly when Matthew glared at her. 'You won't! Won't-won't-won't-'

Jumping out of bed, Matthew pulled her away, but she danced round, chanting at the top of her voice.

'Won't-won't-won't-'

Dad looked in, with his hands over his ears. 'Can't you turn her off, Matthew?'

'No, he can't!' shrieked Emily. 'I haven't

got a tap! Won't-won't-won't-'

'No tap?' Dad winked at Matthew. Then he caught hold of Emily and parted her hair at the back. 'Oh yes you have. Hasn't she, Matt?'

Matthew winked back. 'A little silver tap.'

'Won't-' said Emily. But she didn't sound so certain.

Dad twisted his fingers gently against her scalp. 'It's rather stiff, but I think I can turn it off.'

'Won't-' said Emily, faintly. She wriggled round, trying to look at the back of her head.

'Almost there.' Dad gave his fingers a last twist and stepped back, rubbing his hands. 'Done it!'

Emily stopped chanting. 'A *real* tap?' she whispered.

'We-ell . . .'

Dad was very solemn, but Matthew couldn't keep it up. He started giggling. Emily screeched, and Dad jumped on them both and tickled them all the way downstairs.

'What was all that "won't-ing" about?' he said, as he got out the breakfast things.

Matthew glared at Emily. 'She says she's going to play with my spaceship when I'm at school. And she will. She only left it alone

yesterday because –'

Matthew stopped. She'd left it alone because she went to the library. To be the same as him. So today –

That was *it*! He grabbed Emily's arm.

'Hey, Emily! How about doing some school work? Like me. School work's better than spaceships.'

Emily looked suspicious. '*Real* school work?'

'Yes. We'll ask Mrs Barton what I'm going to do. And you can do it too.'

Emily liked that. She raced upstairs to dress and, all the way to school, she ran ahead of Matthew and Dad. By the time they got into the classroom, she was already talking to Mrs Barton.

'I want to do the same as Matthew. Because Matthew says school work's better than spaceships.'

'Ssh!' Matthew hissed.

He went pink, but Mrs Barton gave him an enormous smile. 'Thank you, Matthew. I hope you like today, too.'

'But what's he going to *do*?' Emily said.

'He's going to make a picture of his family.'

'Me?' said Emily. 'And Mum and Dad and Matthew?'

'That's right.'

Emily beamed. 'I can do that too. I'll do a painting, and bring it at home time, so you can see.' She grabbed Dad's hand, and waved goodbye to Matthew.

Matthew was going to paint his picture, too, but when Mrs Barton handed out the paper, after playtime, Jason headed for the painting corner. He snatched an apron out of Laura's hand and started off with a great orange splash, on the paper and all over his shoes.

'That's my hair!' he said loudly.

Matthew thought he would be safer using pencils. He sat down next to David and began to draw Dad, in his blue jumper and brown trousers.

David was having trouble with his picture. He drew one face, but he didn't like that, so he turned the paper over and drew on the other side. Then he looked at Matthew's.

'That's good.'

Matthew looked back. David's paper was full up. 'You've got a lot of people in your family.'

'Nine,' said David proudly. He pointed. 'Mum. Dad. Kevin and Johnny. Sarah and Lucy and Anne and Amy. One, two, three, four, five, six, seven, eight –'

He stopped.

'What's the matter?' Matthew said.

David frowned. 'There's only eight. But I've done Mum and Dad. And two brothers and four sisters. Who have I forgotten?'

'Maybe you counted wrong,' Matthew said. 'One, two . . .' But he couldn't find nine people either.

Then Jason charged across the room, waving his painting. 'I finished first!' He looked over Matthew's shoulder and snorted. 'That's a silly picture. You've drawn your Mum bigger than your Dad.'

'My Mum *is* bigger than my Dad,' Matthew said.

'Can't be,' Jason said. He leaned over and

looked at David's picture. 'That's wrong too! We're supposed to draw our families. You've done millions of people.'

'They *are* his family,' Matthew said.

David nodded. 'Mum and Dad. Kevin and Johnny. And those four there are my sisters.'

'See?' said Matthew. 'He hasn't done it wrong.'

For a moment, Jason looked cross. Then his eyes lit up. 'Yes he has! The paper's full up – and he hasn't done himself!'

Matthew and David looked at each other. *Oh*, went David's mouth.

'You forgot yourself!' Jason shouted. Everyone turned to stare and David went bright red.

'He *didn't*!' Matthew said, fiercely.

Jason grinned. 'If he didn't forget, where is he?'

'He's – he's –' Matthew thought desperately. 'He's at school, of course!'

'At *school*?'

'Yes.' Whisking the paper over, Matthew pointed at the face that David had drawn first. 'There he is.'

He and David looked at each other, and started to giggle. Jason stamped off, but he looked very cross.

Chapter 4

Tuesday

A Tap on the Head

After lunch, Mrs Barton went round writing names on their pictures. *Matthew* she wrote on Matthew's. *Dad. Mum. Emily.*

'Watch how I do it,' she said. 'And then go over my writing.'

Jason snorted. 'That's *peasy*! I've only got three names to do.'

He finished before everyone else, and Mrs Barton let him choose what to do. He went to the back of the class and began playing with the big wooden building bricks.

When Matthew finished, he went over to join in. But Jason wouldn't let him.

'*I'm* playing with these,' he said, and he glared, to show he hadn't forgotten about being laughed at.

Matthew trailed back to the table and got out a jigsaw, but that was boring, so he went to find David.

'Do you want to play with the Lego?'

David shook his head. 'I can't. I haven't done my writing.' He bent over his paper, and went on copying. *Kevin. Sarah. Amy* . . .

Matthew went back to the jigsaw, looking enviously at Jason. *I'm going to play with those big bricks tomorrow*, he thought. *I'll tell Mum to ask Mrs Barton*.

But when he saw Mum, he forgot all about it. Because Emily came racing across the playground, flapping a big sheet of paper.

'Look, Matthew! Look! I did us all!'

She'd painted four long, spindly people. Matthew recognised Dad by his dark hair. Mum had a book, and he had his grey school trousers. And Emily –

He frowned. 'What's that grey blob on your head?'

Emily giggled. 'It's my tap, that Dad found.'

'What tap?' said a loud voice from behind. Jason reached over Matthew's shoulder and snatched Emily's painting.

Emily grinned. 'The tap on my head,' she said, proudly.

Jason stared at her. Then he held up the painting, to show everyone in the playground. 'Matthew's sister's daft,' he shouted. 'She thinks she's got a tap on her head.'

'No she doesn't,' Matthew muttered.

'I do!' Emily said fiercely. 'I can have a tap on my head if I like.'

'No you can't.' Jason pulled a face at her. 'You're a baby!'

'I'm not!' Emily said. She stamped on his foot, and Jason went bright purple and pulled her hair.

Matthew looked round frantically, but all the mothers were on the far side of the

playground, and the other children seemed to agree with Jason. *Daft*, they were muttering. And *Thinks she's got a tap on her head.* Matthew didn't know what to do.

But David did. He reached up with one finger and tapped the side of Jason's head, very lightly.

Jason spun round. 'What was that?' he snapped.

'A tap on the head,' David said solemnly.

'A – what?'

'I tapped you on the head,' David said. 'So now *you've* got a tap on the head. Like Emily.' He tapped himself. 'So have I.'

Jason still looked baffled, but Emily giggled. She tapped Matthew's head twice.

'You've got two taps!' she shrieked.

Then David did it to Laura, who was just coming out of school, and Laura did it to Andrew. Everyone was laughing, except for Jason.

He stood in the middle, glaring at them all. 'You're daft,' he said loudly.

But no one took any notice of him. They were all too busy getting taps on their heads.

Chapter 5

Wednesday (handwritten)

Bricks

Matthew was happy when he went to bed that night. But when he woke up the next morning he remembered Jason, and how cross he'd been. Somehow, the thought of Jason's cross face made it hard to get up. And when he got downstairs, he didn't want his cornflakes.

Mum looked at him. 'Is there anything wrong?'

'Jason's silly,' Matthew muttered. But he said it too softly for her to hear, because he didn't want to explain.

Emily heard, though. 'Jason's got a tap on his head,' she said. She giggled, and started to put Pink Teddy's dress on to Sarah-Ann, her new rag doll.

31

'Why are you doing that?' Matthew said. He wanted to stop her talking about Jason.

'I'm making Sarah-Ann smart. Because Gemma's coming to play this afternoon.'

Matthew stopped, with his spoon halfway to his mouth. 'This afternoon? But what about your school work?'

'Don't want any school work today,' Emily said.

'But you must!' Matthew could just imagine what would happen otherwise. Emily and Gemma would go upstairs to the bedroom. Gemma would see the spaceship. And she'd say – she'd say –

He put the spoon down. 'No one's allowed in my spaceship except me!'

'But I want to go in,' Emily said sulkily. 'Gemma *likes* space things.' She stuck out her tongue.

Matthew snatched Sarah-Ann and threw her across the room.

'That's enough!' said Mum. She fetched their coats and began to push Emily's arms into her sleeves. 'Let's go to school. Maybe Emily can get some good ideas for playing with Gemma.'

'I don't want school work,' Emily said.

'It's not all work at school,' said Mum. 'Is

32

it, Matthew?'

Matthew shook his head. 'Sometimes we choose.'

'There you are!' Mum did up Emily's buttons. 'Let's go and see what the choosing things are, then.'

But Emily was still cross. All the way to school, she ignored Matthew and when they got into the classroom she marched straight up to Jason.

'What are you going to do in choosing time?' she asked loudly. 'I want to do the same as you.' She sat down on the carpet next to him and stared defiantly at Matthew.

Jason looked at her. Then he looked at Matthew. A huge grin spread over his face.

'I'm going to build a tower,' he said. 'With the big wooden bricks. I'm going to use them all, and build the tallest tower in the whole world.'

'That's not fair!' Matthew said. 'You had them yesterday!'

Jason grinned. 'Well, Mrs Barton said I could have them again today. Because I want to do something special.'

'*I'm* going to build a tower too,' Emily said. She jumped up and pulled a face at Matthew. 'With Gemma. A huge great big tower.'

She stuck her tongue out and bounced off with Mum, and Matthew walked over to the other side of the class, as far away from Jason as he could get. He sat down next to David.

'Jason's smelly,' he said.

David grinned. 'He says he's going to build the tallest tower in the world.'

'That's what *I* was going to do,' said Matthew.

David looked across at the wooden bricks. 'I've got some bricks like that. They're really slippery. If you build them too high, they fall on top of you. Lego's better, because it sticks together.'

'I bet they wouldn't fall on *me*,' Matthew muttered.

'There's loads and loads of that big Lego in Mrs Barton's box,' David said. 'We could build a *really* tall tower with that.'

Matthew stared at him. Then he turned round and looked at the Lego box. 'Do you think we could build the tallest tower in the whole world?'

If they did that, they'd beat Jason. And Emily.

'We could *try*,' David said slowly. 'When we have Choosing Time.'

Matthew grinned. 'Right, then. That's what we'll do. We'll build the tallest tower of all!'

Chapter 6

The Tallest Tower in the World

All day, Matthew and David and Jason worked as hard as they could. They couldn't choose until their work was done.

Jason finished first. He copied his last writing pattern and raced across to show his paper to Mrs Barton.

'Done it! Can I build my tower now?'

Mrs Barton beamed. 'Yes, you can. Well done, Jason.'

Grinning rudely at Matthew, Jason went into the brick corner and Matthew heard the bricks rattle and clink. A few moments later, Laura gasped.

'Jason! That's really *tall*!'

CRASH! The bricks fell with a loud clatter.

'Look what you made me do!' Jason shouted crossly.

Matthew grinned at David and started his last writing pattern.

By the time they were ready to choose, Jason had built a new tower. It was almost as tall as he was, and he was just stretching up to put another brick on top.

But – CRASH!

Matthew laughed and ran across to the Lego corner. David was right. There was *loads* of big Lego. They could build a tower right up to the ceiling.

But it took time. At first, whenever they looked across the classroom, the wooden tower was much taller than their plastic one. But it kept crashing down again, and all the time the Lego tower grew and grew. Even when it broke, it was easy to mend, because most of the bricks stayed together. Up and up it went, until Matthew had to climb on a chair to reach the top.

'It's bigger than Jason's!' he whispered. '*He* doesn't need a chair.'

Jason heard that. He turned round and saw the Lego tower.

'That's not fair!' he said angrily. 'Lego bricks stick together!'

'So?' Matthew climbed on to the chair with the next brick. 'You could have had the Lego, if you wanted.'

Jason glared, and Matthew thought he was going to knock their tower over. But he didn't. Instead, he ran across the classroom and fetched something from a box near the door. When he came back, he was grinning.

David passed up two more pieces of Lego. 'Those are the last ones. Our tower's as big as it can get.'

'And it's *much* bigger than Jason's!' Matthew said. He added the bricks and turned triumphantly.

But he got a shock.

Jason had been working hard. His tower was taller than ever, and he was standing on a chair too. The other children had stopped work to watch, but he wasn't letting anyone help him. He stood on the chair, with his back to the class, adding brick after brick.

And not one of them slithered down.

David frowned. 'That's impossible. They always fall.'

'Let's go and see what he's doing,' whispered Matthew.

They crept across and looked up at the wooden tower. *It's very, very tall,* Matthew thought gloomily. He watched Jason as he climbed up with another brick – and he saw a brown lump in the palm of his hand.

'Mrs Barton!' he shouted. 'Jason's cheating! He's sticking the bricks together with Plasticine!'

Mrs Barton was helping Lucy with her writing patterns, but she put the pencil down and came across the room.

'I'm not cheating!' Jason said, hotly. '*Real* builders stick their bricks together. And my tower's the tallest, isn't it?'

'We-ell,' Mrs Barton looked at the wooden tower, and then at the Lego one. 'I don't like having Plasticine all over my bricks, but yes, yours is taller.'

'YEAH!' Jason jumped off the chair. 'Can my dad come in and see?'

'All right,' Mrs Barton said. 'After our story.'

The instant the story was over, Jason leaped to his feet and raced into the playground to fetch his father.

Matthew trailed out more slowly. When he got into the playground, his mother wasn't there. She raced in a moment later, on her own, gasping and out of breath.

'I thought – we'd never – make it. Emily

and Gemma are bringing their tower and they're – walking like snails.'

Matthew looked across the playground. Emily and Gemma were just coming in, carrying the tower between them. It was *enormous*. A long line of boxes and cardboard rolls and cereal packets, all stuck together with sellotape.

They stopped in the middle of the playground and put down one end of the tower. Then, very carefully, they lifted the other end, until the tower was standing upright.

It was much, much taller than they were. It was taller than Mum. It reached right to the top of the climbing frame at the back of the playground.

Matthew blinked. Then he saw David coming out of school. And Jason, with his dad.

'Hey!' he yelled. 'Look at my sister's tower!'

Jason stared. 'That's silly!' he said. 'It's –' Then he stopped. He couldn't say *It's stuck.* Because if sticking was silly, his tower was silly too.

Emily tossed her head. 'It's the tallest tower in the world!' she said, in a very loud voice.

Jason looked so furious that Matthew thought, *He's going to smash Emily's tower!*

But then, behind them, a soft voice said, 'The tallest tower in the world?'

Matthew and Jason turned round. There

was David, pointing past them, at the church across the road.

The church tower rose high above them all. Taller than the school. Taller than the flats across the road. It was the biggest thing they could see.

And in front of it, beaming proudly, was Emily, with her little pile of cardboard boxes.

Matthew started to smile.

Sssh, went David's mouth. But it was too late. Jason was smiling as well.

Emily didn't understand, because she had her back to the church. 'What's so funny?' she said. 'My tower's huge! You've never seen a bigger tower in your *whole life*. Have you?'

Matthew couldn't speak, in case he burst out laughing, and David had his hand over his mouth. But Emily wasn't going to give up. She stood glaring at them all, waiting for an answer.

It was Jason who found the right words.

'Don't take any notice of *them*,' he said, scornfully. 'They're just jealous, because your tower's so big. You've beaten us all.'

He sounded just as horrible as usual. But when he turned round, his face wasn't horrible at all. He was grinning at them.

Chapter 7

Thursday

Something Red

On Thursday, they woke up very late. They got ready as fast as they could, but just as Mum opened the front door, Matthew remembered something.

'We can't go yet!'

'Why not?' said Mum, impatiently.

'I've got to have something red.'

'Oh, Matthew, you can't do that now. We'll be late.'

'I've got to. Mrs Barton said we had to bring it today.'

'But there isn't any time –'

'I know something red!' Emily shrieked.

She raced into the kitchen and they heard the fridge door bang. Then she came marching back, proudly carrying the tomato ketchup bottle.

'There you are!'

'*Oh* no,' Mum lifted the bottle out of her hands. 'Matthew's not taking *that* to school. If he must have something red, he'd better find one of his toys.'

'I'll get one,' Matthew said. He tore into the sitting room and began to toss things out of the toy box.

Not Red Ted. His paws were brown. Not the big red bus with the black seats. Or the red

postbox with the blue and yellow and green shapes. Or the jack-in-the-box, or the Father Christmas rattle, or the red-and-black striped snake –

Mum came marching in. 'What are you doing?'

'Looking for something red,' Matthew said, tossing out the flowery plastic teapot and the cuddly ladybird.

'But you've got millions of red things there.'

'Not red all *over*. They've got other colours.'

Mum sighed. 'Does that really matter?'

'Of course it does. Mrs Barton said *red*.' Matthew pulled out the red racing car, and then saw the silver number on its bonnet. He lifted his hand to throw it on the floor.

'Oh no you don't!' Mum said. 'You've made enough mess. I've got a coffee morning in here while Emily's at playgroup. You'll have to tidy up before you go to school.'

'But there isn't time. And I haven't found anything red.'

'*I'll* find you something.' Mum reached in and pulled out a big red brick. 'Is that good enough?'

Matthew looked at it. It was red all over. There wasn't a single spot of any other colour.

Slowly, he nodded.

'Right!' said Mum. 'I'll keep it safe, then.' She put it in her coat pocket. 'Now pick up everything else.'

Matthew looked at the floor. It was covered in almost-red toys. They'd take hours and hours to put back.

'But I can't –' he began. Then he had a brilliant idea. 'If I leave them here, Emily can make an *almost*-red collection while I'm at school. That can be her school work.'

'Not this morning,' said Mum. 'This morning the room has to be clear. Pick up those toys.'

Matthew scrabbled round on his hands and knees, throwing the toys back into the box. It was very late by the time he put in the last one. Even though they ran all the way to school, the children were sitting on the carpet when they got there.

'Hurry!' whispered Mum. She gave Matthew a quick kiss and pushed him towards the others. Then she grabbed Emily's hand.

'Don't forget!' Matthew whispered, as they turned away. 'When Emily gets back from playgroup, she's going to make an almost-red collection.'

'No, I'm not!' Emily said, scowling. 'I want to do the same as you and Jason. I'm going to find *really* red things. And bring them all to school at home time.'

'OK,' muttered Mum. 'As long as you don't bring the tomato ketchup.'

She waved and hauled Emily off, and Matthew went and sat on the carpet, wriggling past Jason to get next to David.

Mrs Barton smiled down at him. 'Well, I know one person who's remembered to bring something red. Well done, Matthew. Who else remembered?'

'Me!' said Jason. 'Look!' He jumped to his feet, holding up a big red plastic bus. Then he sat down again, on Matthew's feet, and waved the bus at him. 'I bet you haven't got anything as good as this.'

'I'm sure Matthew's brought something just as red as your bus,' said Mrs Barton. 'Haven't you, Matthew?'

'Yes, I have,' Matthew said. 'I've got –' He stopped.

'Come on,' Mrs Barton said. 'Let's see.'

But Matthew just stared at her, with his mouth open. Because he hadn't got anything red after all. His mother had gone off with the brick still in her pocket.

Jason guessed, straight away. He chuckled and pushed Matthew on to David's knees. 'You forgot! Didn't you?'

'No, I didn't!' Matthew said, fiercely, clutching Jason's shoulder. 'I remembered. I looked through my toy box and –'

Jason chuckled again and nudged him. 'You forgot!'

'Stop it!' Mrs Barton said. She smiled at Matthew. 'Well?'

'I –' Matthew looked down at the floor. He couldn't say he'd left the brick in Mum's pocket. Jason would laugh even more. But what else could he say?

Then he remembered Emily.

'My sister's bringing my red things,' he said loudly. 'Lots of them. At the end of school.'

Chapter 8

Thursday

What Emily Brought

Jason didn't believe it. 'I bet she won't bring anything!'

'Quietly, Jason,' Mrs Barton said. 'Let's see what everyone else has got.'

There were four buses, six bricks, like the one in Mum's pocket, and two cuddly ladybirds. Ten people hadn't brought anything at all.

Mrs Barton lined everything up on the table beside her. 'Well,' she said. 'We've got lots of things for you to draw — but most of the pictures are going to be the same, aren't they?'

Matthew looked at the buses and bricks and ladybirds. 'My sister's bringing lots of other things,' he said loudly. 'We could draw those tomorrow.'

Mrs Barton smiled. 'What do you think Matthew's sister might bring? What's red?'

Laura and Abigail answered together.

'A pillar box!'

'A postman's van!'

'No!' shouted Jason. 'She'll bring strawberries! Yum, yum!'

That made everyone laugh, and Mrs Barton sent them off to start their drawings. But they were enjoying the game too much to stop. People kept coming up to Matthew and whispering in his ear.

'Is your sister going to bring a red crayon?'

'She could get some radishes.'

'How about a lipstick?'

Jason was the only person who didn't join in. When he passed Matthew, he whispered, 'You forgot, didn't you? Your sister won't bring anything.'

'Yes, she will,' Matthew hissed back.

He didn't much care *what* Emily brought, as long as her bag was full of red things. He'd give them to Mrs Barton for tomorrow – and that would show Jason.

He got his chance even sooner than he expected.

While they were listening to the story, at the

end of the afternoon, there was a loud noise outside the classroom. Feet rattled up the corridor, and a grown-up voice yelled, 'Emily! Come back!'

Emily burst into the classroom, waving a plastic carrier bag.

'I've got the red things!' she panted. 'Like I said.'

Mum raced in behind her, looking hot and embarrassed. 'I'm sorry, Mrs Barton. She just ran inside.'

Mrs Barton closed the story book and beckoned to Emily.

'Well, now you're here, let's see what you've brought. We've spent all day wondering about it.'

Triumphantly, Emily marched across the classroom. Matthew turned round and stuck his tongue out at Jason.

'See? I told you she'd come.'

'I bet she's only got more bricks,' Jason said. 'Or a ladybird.'

Mrs Barton looked at the bag. 'Well, Emily – have you got a ladybird? Or a bus? Or a brick?'

Emily snorted. 'My things are *much* better than that.'

'See?' said Matthew. He pulled a face at

Jason. 'Can we draw Emily's things tomorrow, Mrs Barton?'

'Maybe,' Mrs Barton said cautiously. 'Let's look at them first. What have you got, Emily?'

An enormous grin spread over Emily's face. 'I've got a banana!'

Matthew stared at her. '*A banana?*'

'And a pig!' Emily said, nodding happily. 'And a tin of baked beans!'

'They're not red!' Jason squealed with laughter. 'You don't know your colours, Matthew!'

'It's nothing to do with Matthew!' Emily said, furiously. 'They're my things. And I *do* know my colours. Look!'

She stuck her hand into the bag and pulled out the things she'd brought, putting them on the table next to Jason's bus.

A red banana.

A red plastic pig.

A bright red tin.

She had painted them all over, with thick red paint.

For a moment, there was no sound at all. Everyone was too astonished to speak. But Matthew's face was as red as the banana, and he wanted to crawl under the carpet. He *knew* everyone was going to laugh at him.

Then Jason gave a loud, delighted whoop. 'That's brilliant! Can I draw a red banana tomorrow, Mrs Barton?'

And everyone else started shouting.

'Can I do a red pig?'

'I want to do the beans!'

'I want to do all of them!'

Mrs Barton put her hands over her ears until they stopped yelling. Then she looked at the table again.

'Well, they *are* red,' she said, slowly. 'Yes, you can draw them if you like. But you'll have to do some very special writing underneath.'

Jason grinned. 'How about *Hurrah for Emily?*'

And he pushed Matthew over again. But this time Matthew knew he was just being friendly.

Chapter 9

Friday

Beans

On Friday morning, Matthew almost forgot to give Emily any school work. He remembered just in time, as he was finishing his toast.

'Draw something red,' he said. 'Then get Mum to write what it is, and copy over her letters.'

'Don't want to copy,' Emily said. She banged the spoon down into her cornflakes.

'Oo uh –' Matthew swallowed his mouthful and started again. 'You *must*. Or you won't be doing the same as me.'

'So?' Emily banged the spoon again, but this time Dad saw her.

'Oh no you don't.' He took the plate away

54

and gave Emily a piece of his toast. 'Leave her alone, Matthew.'

'She's stupid,' Matthew said, crossly. He looked at Emily again. 'The best pictures from yesterday are going to be up on the wall.'

Emily looked interested. 'Will your picture be up too?'

'We-ell . . .' Matthew hoped Mrs Barton had chosen his ladybird picture.

'We can look when we get to school,' said Mum. 'Hurry *up*, Emily!'

Matthew left Emily chewing and went upstairs to his spaceship. But he kept wondering whether his picture would be on the wall, and the spaceship hadn't even taken off when it was time to go.

At school, the first person they met was Jason, bouncing around with a huge grin on his face.

'My picture's up. And Mrs Barton says it's very good.'

There were six red pictures on the board, and Jason's was the biggest and brightest of all. It was an enormous scarlet bus, with dozens of windows, and the writing underneath was black and strong.

This is a red bus
by
Jason

Matthew's picture wasn't there.

'That's a silly bus!' Emily said. 'Its wheels are all different sizes.' She looked cheekily up at Jason. 'I could draw a better bus than that.'

Matthew froze, waiting for a furious yell, but Jason just grinned at Emily. 'If you did a bus, I bet it would be really funny.'

'It wouldn't!' Emily stamped her foot. 'I can do buses. And bricks and ladybirds. *And* writing. *And* –'

Jason grinned again. 'And red bananas? And pigs and baked beans?'

'Yes!' Emily said. 'I can do them better than you!' She grabbed hold of Mum's hand and pulled it hard. 'Hurry up. I've got to get home and do my work.'

As she stomped off, Jason chuckled. 'Your sister's mad, Matthew.'

'No, she's not,' Matthew said, loyally. 'She's really good at drawing.'

He didn't mean *better than you* – but Jason must have thought he did, because he didn't wander round the class annoying people. He sat very still, drawing the banana and the cow, as carefully as he could.

Matthew did a painting. He wanted it to be really good – good enough to go up on the wall – so he chose the tin of beans, because it looked easy.

But it wasn't. When he'd finished, the tin was just a huge red blob, in the middle of the paper. And when he took it across to Mrs Barton, she said, 'Good try, Matthew,' and wrote

This is a red brick

saying the words out loud as she wrote them down.

'It's not a brick,' Matthew said, miserably. 'It's a tin of beans.'

Mrs Barton rubbed out the words and wrote

This is a red tin of beans

instead. But that didn't help. Because the blob *did* look like a brick. Matthew walked over to

the waste paper basket with the picture and
started to screw it up.

'Don't do that,' David said. 'You'll spoil it.'

Matthew scowled. 'It's stupid. It doesn't
look like a tin of beans at all.'

David stared at it for a moment. Then he
walked across to the table where the red
things were, and stood next to Jason, gazing
at Emily's baked bean tin.

Jason looked up. 'What are you doing?'

Matthew pulled a face, meaning *Don't tell*!,
but David was thinking too hard to notice.
'How can Matthew make his blob look like
that tin?' he said.

Jason looked at the painting. Then he
looked at the tin. 'Beans,' he said.

Chapter 10

Friday

Up on the Wall

Matthew blinked. 'Beans?'

Jason nodded. 'Look. You can see them through the paint.'

'But there's *hundreds*.' Matthew stared at the tin. 'If I do them all, my picture'll be full of black lines.'

'Not if you do the lines in red.' David picked up a red crayon and drew a tiny red circle on the dry paint. 'Look. Now your tin's got one bean in.'

Jason chuckled and grabbed another crayon. 'Two!' he said, drawing a circle at the bottom.

Matthew joined in. 'Three!'

'Four!'

59

'Five!'

By the time they got up to twenty, everyone was crowding round, counting.

'Twenty-one!'

'Twenty-two!'

'Twenty-three!'

When they got stuck at sixty-nine, Mrs Barton came to help, and they went on until there wasn't room for any more beans. There were a hundred and fifty-seven of them.

'Well!' said Mrs Barton. 'This is a very special picture. I think it needs some extra writing.'

Very carefully, she wrote two more lines under the picture. Now it said

This is a red tin of beans
by Matthew and David and Jason.
There are 157 beans.

'Copy over the letters,' she said. 'Then I'll put it up on the wall.'

And she did. Right in the middle of the board.

Matthew could hardly wait to tell Mum. As soon as they came out of school, he charged across the playground with David and Jason.

'We did a really good picture! Of a tin with a hundred and fifty-seven baked beans! And it's up on the wall!'

Mum gave him a big hug, and smiled at Jason and David. 'Well done! You *must* have worked hard!'

Jason looked at Emily. 'I've got two pictures up now,' he said. 'I bet you yours aren't as good as mine.'

'Yes, they are!' Emily said. 'Mine are up on the wall too. You'll have to come to our house if you want to see them.'

'Up on the wall?' Mum said.

She looked puzzled, but Matthew didn't take any notice. He tugged at her arm.

'*Can* they come to our house? Please, Mum! To play.'

'Mmm?' Mum looked vague. 'All right. If their parents don't mind.'

A few moments later they were all walking down the road together, and Emily was chattering non-stop.

'*I've* got pictures up too. *And* writing, just like you. Only my pictures are better.'

'Bet they're not!' Jason said.

'Bet they are!' shouted Emily.

The moment they got home, she darted inside.

'Come upstairs and I'll show you!'

Matthew, David and Jason rattled up the stairs behind her and she flung the bedroom door open.

'There you are! Look!'

They stared.

The pictures certainly were up on the wall. All over. She had drawn them straight on to the wallpaper, with thick red crayon. And round them, in black crayon, she had written squiggles and shapes a bit like letters.

Jason looked awed. 'Are you *allowed* to do that?'

'No, she isn't!' said Mum. She was standing behind them, looking quite pale. 'Emily, you naughty, *naughty* girl! Your bedroom's only just been decorated.'

'They're quite nice pictures,' said David.

'They're brilliant!' Emily shouted. 'That's my bus. And my bananas and my cow and my brick and my tin of beans –'

'You haven't drawn the beans on the tin,' Jason said. 'It's not *nearly* as good as ours!'

Mum took a long, deep breath. 'Well, why don't you three draw the beans while I have a long, serious talk with Emily?'

She marched Emily off, and David looked at Matthew. 'D'you think she really meant that?'

'Don't see why not,' Matthew said. 'Emily's ruined the walls already.'

'Come on, then!' Jason yelled. 'Let's draw beans! And then we'll play with that spaceship thing! OK?'

For a second, Matthew hesitated. Then he grinned. 'OK! We can fly to the moon!'

The beans didn't take long to draw, and the spaceship game was so good that they all forgot all about Emily. But at bedtime, when Dad came to say goodnight, he leaned over the bed and whispered in Matthew's ear.

'Don't you think Emily might be a bit young for real school work?'

'We-ell . . .'

Matthew looked at his spaceship. He thought about Emily and the pictures on the walls.

'It's getting a bit hard, thinking of things for her to do,' he said slowly. 'And anyway –' He thought about drawing the beans. 'And anyway, she can't do proper school work on her own. You need other people.'

He turned over and snuggled down. He couldn't wait for school on Monday. And coming home would be good too.

It was going to be fun seeing what Emily got up to. While he wasn't there.